Dear Parent:
Your child's love of reading starts here!

Every child learns to read in a different way and at his or her own speed. Some go back and forth between reading levels and read favorite books again and again. Others read through each level in order. You can help your young reader improve and become more confident by encouraging his or her own interests and abilities. From books your child reads with you to the first books he or she reads alone, there are I Can Read Books for every stage of reading:

SHARED READING
Basic language, word repetition, and whimsical illustrations, ideal for sharing with your emergent reader

BEGINNING READING
Short sentences, familiar words, and simple concepts for children eager to read on their own

READING WITH HELP
Engaging stories, longer sentences, and language play for developing readers

READING ALONE
Complex plots, challenging vocabulary, and high-interest topics for the independent reader

ADVANCED READING
Short paragraphs, chapters, and exciting themes for the perfect bridge to chapter books

I Can Read Books have introduced children to the joy of reading since 1957. Featuring award-winning authors and illustrators and a fabulous cast of beloved characters, I Can Read Books set the standard for beginning readers.

A lifetime of discovery begins with the magical words **"I Can Read!"**

Visit www.icanread.com for information
on enriching your child's reading experience.

I Can Read Book® is a trademark of HarperCollins Publishers.

Danny and the Dinosaur: Too Tall
Copyright © 2015 by Anti-Defamation League Foundation, Inc., The Authors Guild Foundation, Inc., ORT America, Inc.,
United Negro College Fund, Inc.

Library of Congress Control Number: 2014960372
ISBN 978-0-06-228156-2 (trade bdg.)—ISBN 978-0-06-228155-5 (pbk.)

David Cutting and Rick Farley used Adobe Photoshop to create the digital illustrations for this book.
Typography by Jeff Shake

15 16 17 18 19   SCP   10 9 8 7 6 5 4 3 2 1   ❖   First Edition

I Can Read!

BEGINNING READING **1**

Syd Hoff's

DANNY AND THE DINOSAUR

Too Tall

Written by Bruce Hale

Illustrated in the style of Syd Hoff by David Cutting

HARPER

An Imprint of HarperCollinsPublishers

Danny's dinosaur friend was sad.

"What's wrong?" Danny asked.

"It's not easy being different,"

said the dinosaur.

"I don't get it,"
Danny told him.
"Everyone loves dinosaurs."

"And I love being a dinosaur,"
said the dinosaur.

"But that's not my problem."

"Then what's wrong?" said Danny.

The dinosaur sighed.

"I'm just too tall," he said.

"When I lie in bed,
everything sticks out,"
said the dinosaur.

9

"When I go through doors,"

said the dinosaur,

"it's no fun at all."

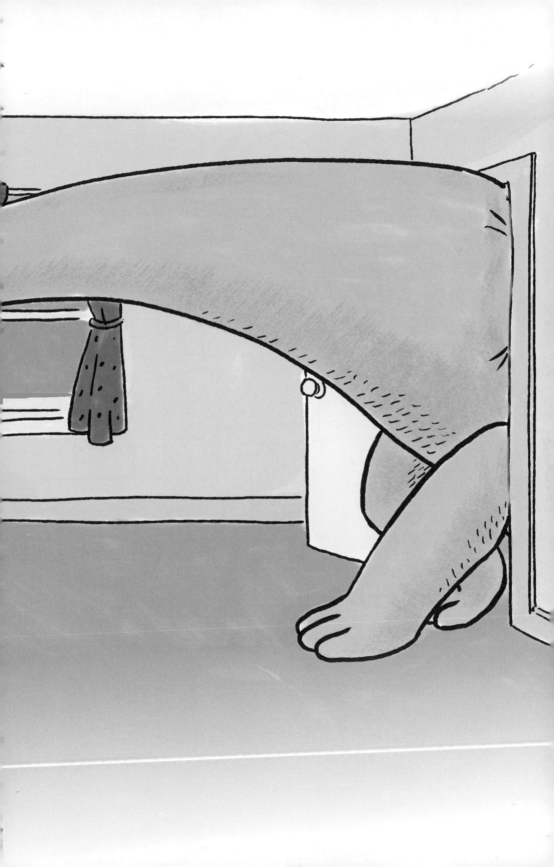

"People ask, 'How's the weather
up there?'" said the dinosaur.

"When I meet new people,
it's hard to say hello."

"Wow," said Danny.

"I had no clue."

The dinosaur nodded.

"Being tall isn't all sunshine

and rainbows," he said.

And the dinosaur hung his head.

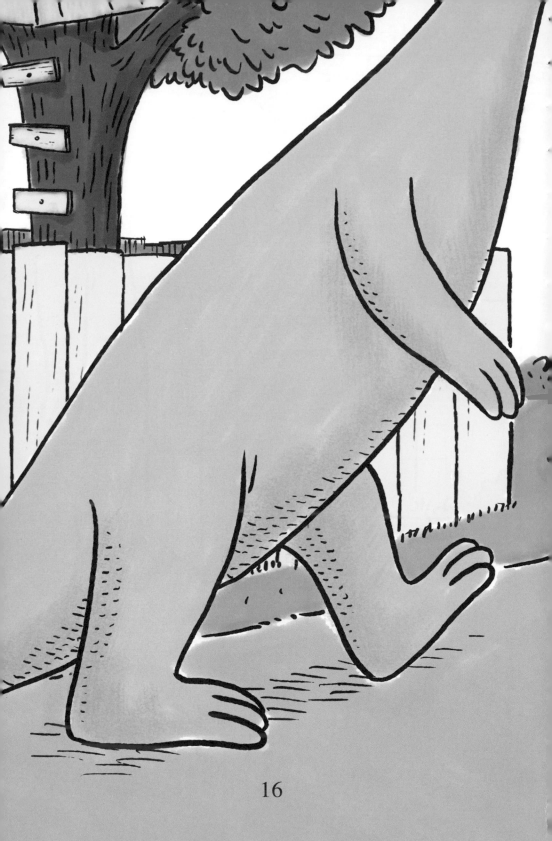

"I know what you need," said Danny.

"Come with me!"

And he took the dinosaur for a walk.

"See?" said Danny.

"Elephants are tall, too."

"Not very tall," said the dinosaur.

"Giraffes are tall like you,"

said Danny.

The dinosaur shook his head.

"Nobody's tall like me."

They left the zoo and walked along.

Then the dinosaur saw a man
at his own eye level!
"Wait," he said. "Who's that?"

"Hello," said the dinosaur.

"How's the weather up there?"

"Just fine," said the man.

"I can see for miles."

Danny and the dinosaur
watched the man work,
lifting heavy things.
But then . . .

. . . the wind gusted,
and the crane swayed.
The man was in danger!

"Help him!" someone yelled.

"He can't get down!"

Danny and the dinosaur came closer.

The dinosaur stretched out his neck.

"Hold on to me," he said.

The man grabbed on . . .

. . . and the dinosaur took him
safely to the ground.

"Lucky thing you showed up,"
said the man. "Thank you!"
The dinosaur smiled.
"What is it?" said Danny.

"I've changed my mind,"

said the dinosaur.

"Being tall is great after all."